Originally published as *Zaza viert feest* in Belgium and Holland by Clavis Uitgeverij, Hasselt—Amsterdam, 2009
English translation from the Dutch by Clavis Publishing Inc., New York

Visit us on the Web at www.clavisbooks.com.

Celebrate with Zaza written and illustrated by Mylo Freeman

ISBN 978-1-60537-376-8

This book was printed in January 2018 at Wai Man Book Binding (China) Ltd. Flat A, 9/F., Phase 1,
Kwun Tong Industrial Centre, 472-484 Kwun Tong Road, Kwun Tong, Kowloon, H.K.

First Edition
10 9 8 7 6 5 4 3 2 1

Clavis Publishing supports the First Amendment and celebrates the right to read.

MYLO FREEMAN

Celebrate with Zaza

Clavis

NEW YORK

Today is Rosie's birthday.
Zaza wants to celebrate!

Rosie sits in the birthday chair.
Zaza makes a special crown for her to wear.

All of Zaza's animal friends
are here to celebrate too.
Look! They have a present for Rosie.

Let's sing the birthday song.
"Happy birthday to you,
happy birthday to you,
happy birthday, dear Rosie,
happy birthday to you."

Time for cake and tea!

Zaza pours tea for all of Rosie's friends.

But wait a minute.

Bobby is here. And George Giraffe. And Mo.

But where is Pinkie?

Pinkie is missing Rosie's party.

Rosie misses Pinkie.

But the party must go on.

Time to open the present.

Zaza helps Rosie, and everyone looks inside the box. What's that?

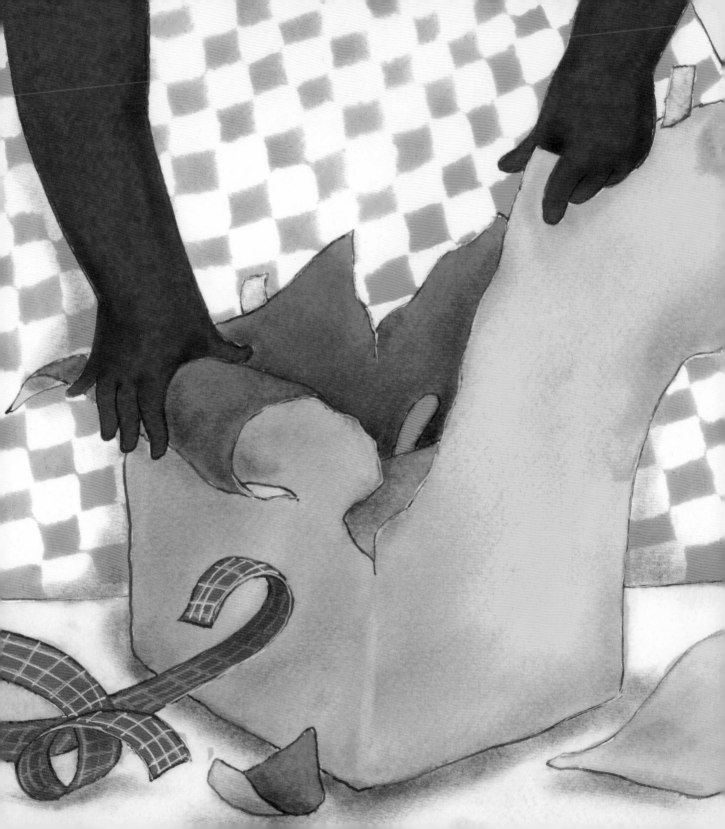

It's Pinkie!

Pinkie is Rosie's present!

Now everyone is here to celebrate.

Happy birthday, Rosie!